There are around 5000 different species of ladybird in the world.

Ladybirds can be red, orange, yellow, black, brown, white, grey, pink or even blue!

In many countries, ladybirds are symbols of good luck, particularly for farmers.

Depending on their species, ladybirds can have spots...

stripes...

...or no markings at all.

Their bright colours warn predators that they are toxic and taste disgusting!

In a big, bustling town lives a girl who loves bugs,
from earthworms to ladybirds, woodlice to slugs.
Her name? Betsy Buglove. It suits her, it's true.
If you were an insect, then she'd love you too!
Yes, Betsy is truly a real nature lover.
She'll show you a world of new friends to discover.

On a chill, windy morning, one crisp autumn day, the children were wrapping up warm to go play.

A carpet of crunchy leaves covered the ground.

Loud, billowing gusts sent them flying around.

As Betsy and Stan pulled their coats on, they saw . . .

... a cluster of ladybirds, twenty or more!

"Up there, by the window!" Stan cried.

"Clumped together. Perhaps they've flown in to hide out from bad weather?

Could you use your **magical glass** to find out why these bugs are inside? What's that all about?"

So, Betsy peered up at the bugs, "What's the matter?"
And that's when the ladybirds started to **chatter!**

"In springtime and summer, it's our job, you know,
to get rid of greenfly, so crops and plants grow."

"In autumn and winter, our work is all done.
We hibernate till the return of the sun."

"We'd just got warmed-up in a big pile of leaves, then WHOOSH! The wind blew like you wouldn't believe!"

"So, we crept through a crack to this warm place to hide . . ."

"...but all of our friends are still freezing outside! The woodlice and lacewings! The spiders and bees!

They're out in the cold still. Can you help us please?"

Betsy thought, "Well . . . we could take your friends inside, too?"

"No way!" cried the ladybirds. "That just won't do!

We'll all wake too soon if we're too warm in there. With no food to eat, we'll go hungry, we fear!"

"Aha!" Betsy cried. "I have thought of a plan. Remember our bug hotel, back at school, Stan?"

"Let's build one right here – make **another** hotel.
We'll just need supplies . . . and the bugs' help as well."

"Our friends can muck in!" Stan grinned. "Let's work together, to make sure the insects are **safe** from bad weather."

So, the spiders led Stan to some pine cones. "Look! Lots!"

While Betsy collected some old garden pots.

"This moss will be cosy!" the young lacewings said.

"On top of those twigs, it's the perfect bug bed!"

"Those hollow bamboo canes make great bee-sized holes."

"And dry leaves and wood will both keep out the cold."

"**Let's build,**" Betsy said, "somewhere sheltered and flat."

"Beneath that tall tree?" asked Stan. "How about that?"

They worked as a **team** and their task was soon done.
"High five!" shouted Stan. "Building that was great fun!"

"And now for our ladybird friends," Betsy said.
"Let's move them outside to their cosy new bed."

They checked Betsy's bug book to see what to do. "We'll just need a cup and a soft paintbrush, too."

Then, gently and slowly, with oodles of care,

they moved all the ladybirds back outside where . . .

"Ta da!" Betsy cried.

"Why, thanks!" said the ladybirds. "Let's go inside!"

"We'll sleep through the winter and then when it's spring, we'll wake up to warmth and the plants it'll bring."

Before long, the bugs settled in their hotel.
"Oh, phew!" Betsy smiled. "I'm so glad that went well."

"Sweet dreams, then!" she called. But there wasn't a peep.

For each tiny insect was now . . .

fast asleep!

For Frankie and his lucky
ladybird, Charlie – C.J.

For Ffion – L.F.

Published in the UK by Scholastic, 2026
Scholastic, Bosworth Avenue, Warwick, CV34 6UQ
Scholastic Ireland, 89E Lagan Road, Dublin Industrial Estate, Glasnevin, Dublin, D11 HP5F

SCHOLASTIC and associated logos are trademarks and/or
registered trademarks of Scholastic Inc.

Text © Catherine Jacob, 2026
Illustrations © Lucy Fleming, 2026

The moral rights of Catherine Jacob and Lucy Fleming have been asserted by them.

HB ISBN 978 0702 34560 9
PB ISBN 978 0702 33132 9

A CIP catalogue record for this book is available from the British Library.

All rights reserved.

This book is sold subject to the condition that it shall not, by way of trade or otherwise, be lent, hired out or otherwise circulated in any form of binding or cover other than that in which it is published. No part of this publication may be reproduced, stored in a retrieval system, or transmitted in any form or by any other means (electronic, mechanical, photocopying, recording or otherwise) or used to train any artificial intelligence technologies without prior written permission of Scholastic Limited. Subject to EU law Scholastic Limited expressly reserves this work from the text and data mining exception.

Printed in China

Paper made from wood grown in sustainable forests and other controlled sources.

1 3 5 7 9 10 8 6 4 2

This is a work of fiction. Any resemblance to actual people, events or locales is entirely coincidental.

Scholastic does not have any control over and does not assume any responsibility for
any third-party websites or other platforms, or their content.

www.scholastic.co.uk

For safety or quality concerns:
UK: www.scholastic.co.uk/productinformation
EU: www.scholastic.ie/productinformation

Ladybirds can survive without fresh air for a full hour underwater!

Ladybirds have the power to smell with their feet, through tiny, hair-like structures.

Ladybirds have very powerful antennae that can detect changes in temperature.